A·TREASURY·OF FLOWER·FAIRIES

A·TREASURY·OF FLOWER·FAIRIES

PLANTAIN AND MOON-DAISY DANCING TOGETHER,
ALL·THROUGH THE·BEAUTIFUL·SUNSHINY·WEATHER

Poems and pictures by

CICELY MARY BARKER

◆

FREDERICK WARNE

*The reproductions in this book have been made using the most
modern electronic scanning methods from entirely new transparencies
of Cicely Mary Barker's original watercolours. They enable Cicely Mary Barker's skill as an artist
to be appreciated as never before.*

The original illustrations of the Windflower Fairy, the Lady's Smock Fairy, the Dandelion Fairy,
the Stitchwort Fairy, the Daffodil Fairy, the Daisy Fairy and the Dead-nettle Fairy have been
lost so a first edition has been used to reproduce these pictures.

FREDERICK WARNE

Published by the Penguin Group
27 Wrights Lane, London W8 5TZ, England
Penguin Books USA Inc., 375 Hudson Street, New York, New York 10014, USA
Penguin Books Australia Ltd, Ringwood, Victoria, Australia
Penguin Books Canada Ltd, 2801 John Street, Markham, Ontario, Canada L3R 1B4
Penguin Books (NZ) Ltd, 182-190 Wairau Road, Auckland 10, New Zealand

Penguin Books Ltd, Registered Offices: Harmondsworth, Middlesex, England

First published in this format 1991

1 3 5 7 9 10 8 6 4 2

Colour reproduction by Anglia Graphics Ltd, Bedford
Printed and bound in Great Britain by
William Clowes Limited, Beccles and London

◆CONTENTS◆

The Crocus Fairies

◆ THE SONG OF ◆
THE CROCUS FAIRIES

Crocus of yellow, new and gay;
Mauve and purple, in brave array;
    Crocus white
    Like a cup of light,—
Hundreds of them are smiling up,
Each with a flame in its shining cup,
By the touch of the warm and welcome sun
Opened suddenly. Spring's begun!
Dance then, fairies, for joy, and sing
The song of the coming again of Spring

◆ THE SONG OF ◆
THE WINDFLOWER FAIRY

While human-folk slumber,
   The fairies espy
Stars without number
   Sprinkling the sky.

The Winter's long sleeping,
   Like night-time, is done;
But day-stars are leaping
   To welcome the sun.

Star-like they sprinkle
   The wildwood with light;
Countless they twinkle—
   The Windflowers white!

("Windflower" is another name for Wood Anemone.)

The Windflower Fairy

The Dandelion Fairy

◆ THE SONG OF ◆
THE DANDELION FAIRY

Here's the Dandelion's rhyme:
   See my leaves with tooth-like edges;
Blow my clocks to tell the time;
   See me flaunting by the hedges,
In the meadow, in the lane,
   Gay and naughty in the garden;
Pull me up—I grow again,
   Asking neither leave nor pardon.
Sillies, what are you about
   With your spades and hoes of iron?
You can never drive me out—
   Me, the dauntless Dandelion!

◆ THE SONG OF ◆
THE DAFFODIL FAIRY

I'm everyone's darling: the blackbird and
    starling
Are shouting about me from blossoming
    boughs;
For I, the Lent Lily, the Daffy-down-dilly,
Have heard through the country the call to
    arouse.
The orchards are ringing with voices
    a-singing
The praise of my petticoat, praise of my
    gown;
The children are playing, and hark! they are
    saying
That Daffy-down-dilly is come up to town!

The Daffodil Fairy

The Lady's-Smock Fairy

◆ THE SONG OF ◆
THE LADY'S-SMOCK FAIRY

Where the grass is damp and green,
Where the shallow streams are flowing,
Where the cowslip buds are showing,
    I am seen.

Dainty as a fairy's frock,
White or mauve, of elfin sewing,
'Tis the meadow-maiden growing—
    Lady's-smock.

◆ THE SONG OF ◆
THE STITCHWORT FAIRY

I am brittle-stemmed and slender,
But the grass is my defender.

On the banks where grass is long,
I can stand erect and strong.

All my mass of starry faces
Looking up from wayside places,

From the thick and tangled grass,
Gives you greeting as you pass.

(A prettier name for Stitchwort is Starwort, but it is not
so often used.)

The Stitchwort Fairy

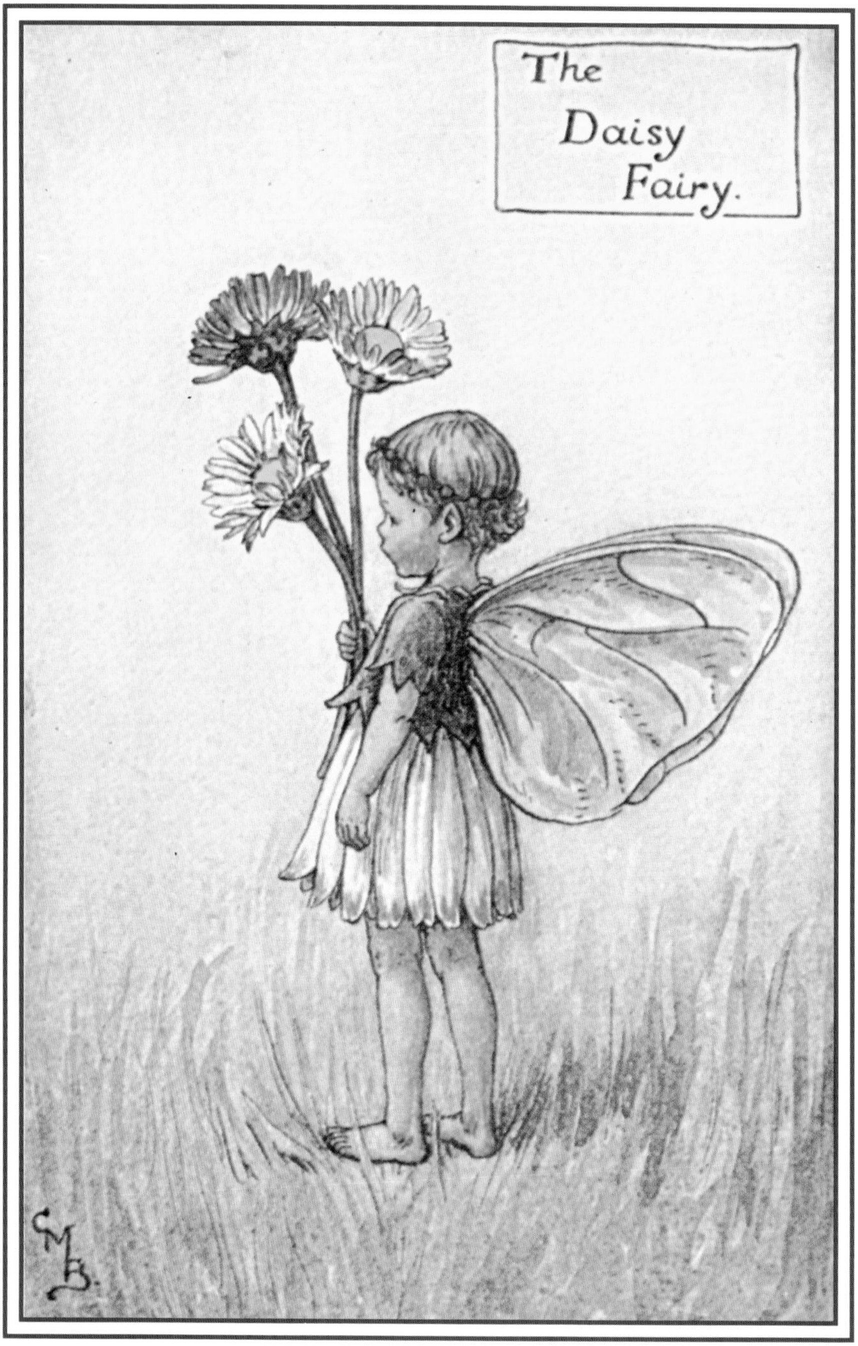

The Daisy Fairy

◆ THE SONG OF ◆
THE DAISY FAIRY

Come to me and play with me,
  I'm the babies' flower;
Make a necklace gay with me,
Spend the whole long day with me,
  Till the sunset hour.

I must say Good-night, you know,
  Till tomorrow's playtime;
Close my petals tight, you know,
Shut the red and white, you know,
  Sleeping till the daytime.

◆ THE SONG OF ◆
THE BUTTERCUP FAIRY

'Tis I whom children love the best;
   My wealth is all for them;
For them is set each glossy cup
   Upon each sturdy stem.

O little playmates whom I love!
   The sky is summer-blue,
And meadows full of buttercups
   Are spread abroad for you.

The Buttercup Fairy

The Forget-me-not Fairy

♦ THE SONG OF ♦
THE FORGET-ME-NOT FAIRY

So small, so blue, in grassy places
 My flowers raise
 Their tiny faces.

By streams my bigger sisters grow,
 And smile in gardens,
 In a row.

I've never seen a garden plot;
 But though I'm small
 Forget me not!

◆ THE SONG OF ◆
THE FOXGLOVE FAIRY

"Foxglove, Foxglove,
　　What do you see?"
The cool green woodland,
　　The fat velvet bee;
Hey, Mr Bumble,
　　I've honey here for thee!

"Foxglove, Foxglove,
　　What see you now?"
The soft summer moonlight
　　On bracken, grass, and bough;
And all the fairies dancing
　　As only they know how.

The Foxglove Fairy

The Wild Rose Fairy

◆ THE SONG OF ◆
THE WILD ROSE FAIRY

I am the queen whom everybody knows:
    I am the English Rose;
As light and free as any Jenny Wren,
    As dear to Englishmen;
As joyous as a Robin Redbreast's tune,
    I scent the air of June;
My buds are rosy as a baby's cheek;
    I have one word to speak,
One word which is my secret and my song,
'Tis "England, England, England" all day long.

◆ THE SONG OF ◆
THE HAREBELL FAIRY

O bells, on stems so thin and fine!
    No human ear
    Your sound can hear,
O lightly chiming bells of mine!

When dim and dewy twilight falls,
    Then comes the time
    When harebells chime
For fairy feasts and fairy balls.

They tinkle while the fairies play,
    With dance and song,
    The whole night long,
Till daybreak wakens, cold and grey,
And elfin music fades away.

(The Harebell is the Bluebell of Scotland.)

The Harebell Fairy

The Toadflax Fairy

◆ THE SONG OF ◆
THE TOADFLAX FAIRY

The children, the children,
    they call me funny names,
They take me for their darling
    and partner in their games;
They pinch my flowers' yellow mouths,
    to open them and close,
Saying, *Snap-Dragon!*
      Toadflax!
        or, *darling Bunny-Nose!*

The Toadflax, the Toadflax,
    with lemon-coloured spikes,
With funny friendly faces
    that everybody likes,
Upon the grassy hillside
    and hedgerow bank it grows,
And it's *Snap-Dragon !*
      Toadflax!
        and *darling Bunny-Nose!*

◆ THE SONG OF ◆
THE SCABIOUS FAIRY

Like frilly cushions full of pins
For tiny dames and fairykins;

Or else like dancers decked with gems,
My flowers sway on slender stems.

They curtsey in the meadow grass,
And nod to butterflies who pass.

The Scabious Fairy

The Traveller's Joy Fairy

◆ THE SONG OF ◆
THE TRAVELLER'S JOY FAIRY

Traveller, traveller, tramping by
To the seaport town where the big ships lie,
See, I have built a shady bower
To shelter you from the sun or shower.
Rest for a bit, then on, my boy!
Luck go with you, and Traveller's Joy!

Traveller, traveller, tramping home
From foreign places beyond the foam,
See, I have hung out a white festoon
To greet the lad with the dusty shoon.
Somewhere a lass looks out for a boy:
Luck be with you, and Traveller's Joy!

(Traveller's Joy is Wild Clematis; and when the flowers are
over, it becomes a mass of silky fluff, and then we call it Old-
Man's-Beard.)

◆ THE SONG OF ◆
THE MOUNTAIN ASH FAIRY

They thought me, once, a magic tree
    Of wondrous lucky charm,
And at the door they planted me
    To keep the house from harm.

They have no fear of witchcraft now,
    Yet here am I today;
I've hung my berries from the bough,
    And merrily I say:

"Come, all you blackbirds, bring your wives,
    Your sons and daughters too;
The finest banquet of your lives
    Is here prepared for you."

(The Mountain Ash's other name is Rowan; and it used to
be called Witchentree and Witch-wood too.)

The Mountain Ash Fairy

The Horse Chestnut Fairy

◆ THE SONG OF ◆
THE HORSE CHESTNUT FAIRY

My conkers, they are shiny things,
    And things of mighty joy,
And they are like the wealth of kings
    To every little boy;
I see the upturned face of each
    Who stands around the tree:
He sees his treasure out of reach,
    But does not notice *me*.

For love of conkers bright and brown,
    He pelts the tree all day;
With stones and sticks he knocks them down,
    And thinks it jolly play.
But sometimes I, the elf, am hit
    Until I'm black and blue;
O laddies, only wait a bit,
    I'll shake them down to you!

◆ THE SONG OF ◆
THE NIGHTSHADE BERRY FAIRY

"You see my berries, how they gleam and
　　glow,
Clear ruby-red, and green, and orange-
　　yellow;
Do they not tempt you, fairies, dangling so?"
　　The fairies shake their heads and answer "No!
　　　You are a crafty fellow!"

"What, won't you try them? There is
　　naught to pay!
Why should you think my berries poisoned
　　things?
You fairies may look scared and fly away—
The children will believe me when I say
　　My fruit is fruit for kings!"
　But all good fairies cry in anxious haste,
"*O children, do not taste!"*

(You must believe the good fairies, though the berries look
nice. This is the Woody Nightshade, which has purple and
yellow flowers in the summer.)

The Nightshade Berry Fairy

The Crab-Apple Fairy

♦ THE SONG OF ♦
THE CRAB-APPLE FAIRY

Crab-apples, Crab-apples, out in the wood,
Little and bitter, yet little and good!
The apples in orchards, so rosy and fine,
Are children of wild little apples like mine.

The branches are laden, and droop to the
     ground;
The fairy-fruit falls in a circle around;
Now all you good children, come gather
     them up:
They'll make you sweet jelly to spread
     when you sup.

One little apple I'll catch for myself;
I'll stew it, and strain it, to store on a shelf
In four or five acorn-cups, locked with a key
In a cupboard of mine at the root of the tree.

◆ THE SONG OF ◆
THE HAZEL-NUT FAIRY

Slowly, slowly, growing
   While I watched them well,
See, my nuts have ripened;
   Now I've news to tell.
I will tell the Squirrel,
   "Here's a store for you;
But, kind Sir, remember
   The Nuthatch likes them too."

I will tell the Nuthatch,
   "Now, Sir, you may come;
Choose your nuts and crack them,
   But leave the children some."
I will tell the children,
   "You may take your share;
Come and fill your pockets,
   But leave a few to spare."

The Hazel-Nut Fairy

The Hawthorn Fairy

◆ THE SONG OF ◆
THE HAWTHORN FAIRY

These thorny branches bore the May
    So many months ago,
That when the scattered petals lay
    Like drifts of fallen snow,
      "This is the story's end," you said;
    But O, not half was told!
For see, my haws are here instead,
And hungry birdies shall be fed
    On these when days are cold.

◆ THE SONG OF ◆
THE SLOE FAIRY

When Blackthorn blossoms leap to sight,
They deck the hedge with starry light,
    In early Spring
    When rough winds blow,
    Each promising
    A purple sloe.

And now is Autumn here, and lo,
The Blackthorn bears the purple sloe!
    But ah, how much
    Too sharp these plums,
    Until the touch
    Of Winter comes!

(The sloe is a wild plum. One bite will set your teeth on
edge until it has been mellowed by frost; but it is not poisonous.)

The Sloe Fairy

The Yew Fairy

◆ THE SONG OF ◆
THE YEW FAIRY

Here, on the dark and solemn Yew,
    A marvel may be seen,
Where waxen berries, pink and new,
    Appear amid the green.

I sit a-dreaming in the tree,
    So old and yet so new;
One hundred years, or two, or three
    Are little to the Yew.

I think of bygone centuries,
    And seem to see anew
The archers face their enemies
    With bended bows of Yew.

◆ THE SONG OF ◆
THE WINTER JASMINE FAIRY

All through the Summer my leaves were green,
But never a flower of mine was seen;
Now Summer is gone, that was so gay,
And my little green leaves are shed away.
      In the grey of the year
      What cheer, what cheer?

The Winter is come, the cold winds blow;
I shall feel the frost and the drifting snow;
But the sun can shine in December too,
And this is the time of my gift to you.
      See here, see here,
      My flowers appear!

The swallows have flown beyond the sea,
But friendly Robin, he stays with me;
And little Tom-Tit, so busy and small,
Hops where the jasmine is thick on the wall;
      And we say: "Good cheer!
      We're here! We're here!"

The Winter Jasmine Fairy

The Dead-Nettle Fairy

◆ THE SONG OF ◆
THE DEAD-NETTLE FAIRY

Through sun and rain, the country lane,
The field, the road, are my abode.
Though leaf and bud be splashed with mud,
Who cares? Not I!—I see the sky,
The kindly sun, the wayside fun
Of tramping folk who smoke and joke,
The bairns who heed my dusty weed
(No sting have I to make them cry),
And truth to tell, they love me well.
My brothers, White, and Yellow bright,
Are finer chaps than I, perhaps;
Who cares? Not I! So now good-bye.

◆ THE SONG OF ◆
THE RUSH-GRASS AND
COTTON-GRASS FAIRIES

Safe across the moorland
   Travellers may go,
If they heed our warning—
   We're the ones who know!

Let the footpath guide you—
   You'll be safely led;
There is bog beside you
   Where you cannot tread!

Mind where you are going!
   If you turn aside
Where you see us growing,
   Trouble will betide.

Keep you to the path, then!
   Hark to what we say!
Else, into the quagmire
   You will surely stray.

The Rush-Grass and
Cotton-Grass Fairies

The Lords-and-Ladies Fairy

◆ THE SONG OF ◆
THE LORDS-AND-LADIES FAIRY

Fairies, when you lose your way,
   From the dance returning,
In the darkest undergrowth
   See my candles burning!
These shall make the pathway plain
Homeward to your beds again.

(These are the berries of the Wild Arum, which has many
other names, and has a flower like a hood in the Spring.
The berries are not to be eaten.)

◆ THE SONG OF ◆
THE PINE TREE FAIRY

A tall, tall tree is the Pine tree,
   With its trunk of bright red-brown—
The red of the merry squirrels
   Who go scampering up and down.

There are cones on the tall, tall Pine tree,
   With its needles sharp and green;
Small seeds in the cones are hidden,
   And they ripen there unseen.

The elves play games with the squirrels
   At the top of the tall, tall tree,
Throwing cones for the squirrels to nibble—
   I wish I were there to see!

The Pine Tree Fairy

The Holly Fairy

◆ THE SONG OF ◆
THE HOLLY FAIRY

O, I am green in Winter-time,
  When other trees are brown;
Of all the trees (So saith the rhyme)
  The holly bears the crown.
December days are drawing near
  When I shall come to town,
And carol-boys go singing clear
Of all the trees (O hush and hear!)
  The holly bears the crown!

For who so well-beloved and merry
As the scarlet Holly Berry?

◆ THE SONG OF ◆
THE WILD CHERRY BLOSSOM

In April when the woodland ways
  Are all made glad and sweet
With primroses and violets
  New-opened at your feet,
    Look up and see
      A fairy tree,
    With blossoms white
      In clusters light,
All set on stalks so slender,
  With pinky leaves so tender.
O Cherry tree, wild Cherry tree!
  You lovely, lovely thing to see!

The Wild Cherry Blossom Fairy

The Laburnum Fairy

◆ THE SONG OF ◆
THE LABURNUM FAIRY

All Laburnum's
Yellow flowers
Hanging thick
In happy showers,—
Look at them!
The reason's plain
Why folks call them
"Golden Rain"!
"Golden Chains"
They call them too,
Swinging there
Against the blue.

(After the flowers, the Laburnum has pods with what look
like tiny green peas in them; but it is best not to play with
them, and they must never, never be eaten, as they are
poisonous.)

◆ THE SONG OF ◆
THE SYCAMORE FAIRY

Because my seeds have wings, you know,
  They fly away to earth;
And where they fall, why, there they grow—
  New Sycamores have birth!
Perhaps a score? Oh, hundreds more!
  Too many, people say!
And yet to me it's fun to see
  My winged seeds fly away.
(But first they must turn ripe and brown,
  And lose their flush of red;
And *then* they'll all go twirling down
  To earth, to find a bed.)

The Sycamore Fairy

The Lime Tree Fairy

◆ THE SONG OF ◆
THE LIME TREE FAIRY

Bees! bees! come to the trees
Where the Lime has hung her treasures;
Come, come, hover and hum;
Come and enjoy your pleasures!
The feast is ready, the guests are bidden;
Under the petals the honey is hidden;
Like pearls shine the drops of sweetness there,
And the scent of the Lime-flowers fills the air.
But soon these blossoms pretty and pale
Will all be gone; and the leaf-like sail
Will bear the little round fruits away;
So bees! bees! come while you may!

The Willow Fairy

◆ THE SONG OF ◆
THE WILLOW FAIRY

By the peaceful stream or the shady pool
I dip my leaves in the water cool.

Over the water I lean all day,
Where the sticklebacks and the minnows play.

I dance, I dance, when the breezes blow,
And dip my toes in the stream below.

◆ THE SONG OF ◆
THE ALDER FAIRY

By the lake or river-side
   Where the Alders dwell,
In the Autumn may be spied
   Baby catkins; cones beside—
Old and new as well.
    Seasons come and seasons go;
That's the tale they tell!

After Autumn, Winter's cold
   Leads us to the Spring;
And, before the leaves unfold,
On the Alder you'll behold,
   Crimson catkins swing!
They are making ready now:
   That's the song I sing!

The Alder Fairy

The Silver Birch Fairy

◆ THE SONG OF ◆
THE SILVER BIRCH FAIRY

There's a gentle tree with a satiny bark,
All silver-white, and upon it, dark,
Is many a crosswise line and mark—
    She's a tree there's no mistaking!
The Birch is this light and lovely tree,
And as light and lovely still is she
When the Summer's time has come to flee,
    As she was at Spring's awaking.

She has new Birch-catkins, small and tight,
Though the old ones scatter
   and take their flight,
And the little leaves, all yellow and bright,
    In the autumn winds are shaking.
And with fluttering wings
   and hands that cling,
The fairies play and the fairies swing
On the fine thin twigs,
   that will toss and spring
    With never a fear of breaking.

◆ THE SONG OF ◆
THE NARCISSUS FAIRY

Brown bulbs were buried deep;
Now, from the kind old earth,
Out of the winter's sleep,
  Comes a new birth!

Flowers on stems that sway;
Flowers of snowy white;
Flowers as sweet as day,
  After the night.

So does Narcissus bring
Tidings most glad and plain:
"Winter's gone; here is Spring—
  Easter again!"

The Narcissus Fairy

◆ THE SONG OF ◆
THE GERANIUM FAIRY

Red, red, vermilion red,
With buds and blooms in a glorious head!
There isn't a flower, the wide world through,
That glows with a brighter scarlet hue.
Her name—Geranium—ev'ryone knows;
She's just as happy wherever she grows,
In an earthen pot or a garden bed—
Red, red, vermilion red!

The Geranium Fairy

The Canterbury Bell Fairy

◆ THE SONG OF ◆
THE CANTERBURY BELL FAIRY

Bells that ring from ancient towers—
    Canterbury Bells—
Give their name to summer flowers—
    Canterbury Bells!
Do the flower-fairies, playing,
Know what those great bells are saying?
    Fairy, in your purple hat,
    Little fairy, tell us that!

"Naught I know of bells in towers—
    Canterbury Bells!
Mine are pink or purple flowers—
    Canterbury Bells!
When I set them all a-swaying,
Something, too, my bells are saying;
Can't you hear them—*ding-dong-ding*—
    Calling fairy-folk to sing?"

◆ THE SONG OF ◆
THE SHIRLEY POPPY FAIRY

We were all of us scarlet, and counted as
    weeds,
  When we grew in the fields with the corn;
Now, fall from your pepper-pots, wee little
    seeds,
  And lovelier things shall be born!

You shall sleep in the soil, and awaken next
    year;
  Your buds shall burst open; behold!
Soft-tinted and silken, shall petals appear,
  And then into Poppies unfold—

Like daintiest ladies, who dance and are gay,
  All frilly and pretty to see!
So I shake out the ripe little seeds, and I say:
  "Go, sleep, and awaken like me!"

(A clergyman, who was also a clever gardener, made these
many-coloured poppies out of the wild ones, and named them
after the village where he was the Vicar.)

The Shirley Poppy Fairy

The Candytuft Fairy

◆ THE SONG OF ◆
THE CANDYTUFT FAIRY

Why am I "Candytuft"?
That I don't know!
Maybe the fairies
First called me so;
Maybe the children,
Just for a joke;
(I'm in the gardens
Of most little folk).

Look at my clusters!
See how they grow:
Some pink or purple,
Some white as snow;
Petals uneven,
Big ones and small;
Not very tufty—
No candy at all!

♦ THE SONG OF ♦
THE GAILLARDIA FAIRY

There once was a child in a garden,
  Who loved all my colours of flame,
The crimson and scarlet and yellow—
  But what was my name?

For *Gaillardia*'s hard to remember!
  She looked at my yellow and red,
And thought of the gold and the glory
  When the sun goes to bed;

And she troubled no more to remember,
  But gave me a splendid new name;
She spoke of my flowers as *Sunsets*—
  Then *you* do the same!

The Gaillardia Fairy

The Sweet Pea Fairies

◆ THE SONG OF ◆
THE SWEET PEA FAIRIES

Here Sweet Peas are climbing;
   (Here's the Sweet Pea rhyme!)
Here are little tendrils,
   Helping them to climb.

Here are sweetest colours;
   Fragrance very sweet;
Here are silky pods of peas,
   Not for us to eat!

Here's a fairy sister,
   Trying on with care
Such a grand new bonnet
   For the baby there.

Does it suit you, Baby?
   Yes, I really think
Nothing's more becoming
   Than this pretty pink!

◆ THE SONG OF ◆
THE JACK-BY-THE-HEDGE FAIRY

"'Morning, Sir, and how-d'ye-do?
   'Morning, pretty lady!"
That is Jack saluting you,
   Where the lane is shady.

Don't you know him? Straight and tall—
   Taller than the nettles;
Large and light his leaves; and small
   Are his buds and petals.

Small and white, with petals four,
   See his flowers growing!
If you never knew before,
   There is Jack for knowing!

(Jack-by-the-hedge is also called Garlic Mustard, and
Sauce Alone.)

The Jack-by-the-hedge Fairy

The Ground Ivy Fairy

◆ THE SONG OF ◆
THE GROUND IVY FAIRY

In Spring he is found;
He creeps on the ground;
But someone's to blame
For the rest of his name—
For Ivy he's *not*!
Oh dear, what a lot
Of muddles we make!
It's quite a mistake,
And really a pity
Because he's so pretty;
He deserves a nice name—
Yes, *someone's* to blame!

(But he has some other names, which we do not hear very
often; here are four of them: Robin-run-up-the-dyke,
Runnadyke, Run-away-Jack, Creeping Charlie.)

◆ THE SONG OF ◆
THE BLACK MEDICK FAIRIES

"Why are we called 'Black', sister,
    When we've yellow flowers?"
"I will show you why, brother:
    See these seeds of ours?
Very soon each tiny seed
    Will be turning black indeed!"

The Black Medick Fairies

The Ribwort Plantain Fairy

◆ THE SONG OF ◆
THE RIBWORT PLANTAIN FAIRY

Hullo, Snailey-O!
How's the world with *you*?
Put your little horns out;
Tell me how you do?
There's rain, and dust, and sunshine,
Where carts go creaking by;
You like it wet, Snailey;
I like it dry!

Hey ho, Snailey-O,
I'll whistle you a tune!
I'm merry in September
As e'er I am in June.
By any stony roadside
Wherever you may roam,
All the summer through, Snailey,
Plantain's at home!

(There are some other kinds of Plantain besides this. The
one with wide leaves, and tall spikes of seed which canaries
enjoy, is Greater Plantain.)

◆ THE SONG OF ◆
THE FUMITORY FAIRY

Given me hundreds of years ago,
My name has a meaning you shall know:
It means, in the speech of the bygone folk,
"Smoke of the Earth" —a soft green smoke!

A wonderful plant to them I seemed;
Strange indeed were the dreams they dreamed,
Partly fancy and partly true,
About "Fumiter" and the way it grew.

Where men have ploughed
    or have dug the ground,
Still, with my rosy flowers, I'm found;
Known and prized by the bygone folk
As "Smoke of the Earth" —
    a soft green smoke!

(The name "Fumitory" was "Fumiter" 300 years ago;
and long before that, "Fume Terre", which is the French
name, still, for the plant. "Fume" means "smoke", "terre"
means "earth".)

The Fumitory Fairy

The Chicory Fairy

◆ THE SONG OF ◆
THE CHICORY FAIRY

By the white cart-road,
  Dusty and dry,
Look! there is Chicory,
  Blue as the sky!

Or, where the footpath
  Goes through the corn,
See her bright flowers,
  Each one new-born!

Though they fade quickly,
  O, have no sorrow!
There will be others
  New-born tomorrow!

(Chicory is also called Succory.)

◆ THE SONG OF ◆
THE JACK-GO-TO-BED-
AT-NOON FAIRY

I'll be asleep by noon!
Though bedtime comes so soon,
  I'm busy too.
Twelve puffs!—and then from sight
I shut my flowers tight;
Only by morning light
  They're seen by you.

Then, on some day of sun,
They'll open wide, each one,
  As something new!
Shepherd, who minds his flock,
Calls it a Shepherd's Clock,
Though it can't say "tick-tock"
  As others do!

(Another of Jack's names, besides Shepherd's Clock is
Goat's Beard.)

The Jack-go-to-bed-at-noon Fairy

The White Bindweed Fairy

◆ THE SONG OF ◆
THE WHITE BINDWEED FAIRY

O long long stems that twine!
O buds, so neatly furled!
O great white bells of mine,
(None purer in the world)
Each lasting but one day!
O leafy garlands, hung
In wreaths beside the way—
Well may your praise be sung!

(But this Bindweed, which is a big sister to the little pink
Field Convolvulus, is not good to have in gardens, though it is
so beautiful; because it winds around other plants and trees.
One of its names is "Hedge Strangler". Morning Glories are
a garden kind of Convolvulus.)

◆ THE SONG OF ◆
THE APPLE BLOSSOM FAIRIES

Up in the tree we see you, blossom-babies,
    All pink and white;
We think there must be fairies to protect you
    From frost and blight,
Until, some windy day, in drifts of petals,
    You take your flight.

You'll fly away! But if we wait with patience,
    Some day we'll find
Here, in your place, full-grown and ripe, the apples
    You left behind—
A goodly gift indeed, from blossom-babies
    To human-kind!

A

Apple Blossom

The Apple Blossom Fairies

Fuchsia

The Fuchsia Fairy

◆ THE SONG OF ◆
THE FUCHSIA FAIRY

Fuchsia is a dancer
Dancing on her toes,
Clad in red and purple,
By a cottage wall;
Sometimes in a greenhouse,
In frilly white and rose,
Dressed in her best for the fairies' evening ball!

(This is the little out-door Fuchsia.)

◆ THE SONG OF ◆
THE IRIS FAIRY

I am Iris: I'm the daughter
Of the marshland and the water.
Looking down, I see the gleam
Of the clear and peaceful stream;
Water-lilies large and fair
With their leaves are floating there;
All the water-world I see,
And my own face smiles at me!

(This is the wild Iris.)

Iris

The Iris Fairy

Jasmine

The Jasmine Fairy

◆ THE SONG OF ◆
THE JASMINE FAIRY

In heat of summer days
With sunshine all ablaze,
Here, here are cool green bowers,
Starry with Jasmine flowers;
Sweet-scented, like a dream
Of Fairyland they seem.

And when the long hot day
At length has worn away,
And twilight deepens, till
The darkness comes—then, still,
The glimmering Jasmine white
Gives fragrance to the night.

◆ THE SONG OF ◆
THE NASTURTIUM FAIRY

Nasturtium the jolly,
  O ho, O ho!
He holds up his brolly
  Just so, just so!
(A shelter from showers,
  A shade from the sun;)
'Mid flame-coloured flowers
  He grins at the fun.
Up fences he scrambles,
  Sing hey, sing hey!
All summer he rambles
  So gay, so gay—
Till the night-frost strikes chilly,
  And Autumn leaves fall,
And he's gone, willy-nilly,
  Umbrella and all.

Nasturtium

The Nasturtium Fairy

Pansy

The Pansy Fairy

◆ THE SONG OF ◆
THE PANSY FAIRY

Pansy and Petunia,
  Periwinkle, Pink—
How to choose the best of them,
Leaving out the rest of them,
  That is hard, I think.

Poppy with its pepper-pots,
  Polyanthus, Pea—
Though I wouldn't slight the rest,
Isn't Pansy *quite* the best,
  Quite the best for P?

Black and brown and velvety,
  Purple, yellow, red;
Loved by people big and small,
All who plant and dig at all
  In a garden bed.

◆ THE SONG OF ◆
THE RAGGED ROBIN FAIRY

In wet marshy meadows
A tattered piper strays—
Ragged, ragged Robin;
On thin reeds he plays.

He asks for no payment;
He plays, for delight,
A tune for the fairies
To dance to, at night.

They nod and they whisper,
And say, looking wise,
"A princeling is Robin,
For all his disguise!

Ragged Robin

The Ragged Robin Fairy